Shopping with Samantha

BY TEDDY SLATER
PICTURES BY DIANE DAWSON HEARN

Silver Press

To patient mothers everywhere, especially my own.
—D.D.H.

For Marcia Longman.
—T.S.

Library of Congress Cataloging-in-Publication Data
Slater, Teddy.
     Shopping with Samantha / by Teddy Slater;
pictures by Diane Dawson Hearn.
        p. cm.—(What rhymes?)
     Summary: After hearing "Don't touch!" several times
during a trip to the department store, Samantha receives a
surprise from her mother. At various points in the text, the
reader is asked to guess which word completes the rhyming verse.
     [1. Shopping—Fiction. 2. Department stores—Fiction.
3. Bears—Fiction. 4. Stories in rhyme. 5. Literary recreations.]
I. Hearn, Diane Dawson, ill.   II. Title.   III. Series.
PZ8.3.S378 Sh   1991
[E]—dc20   90-43550
ISBN 0-671-72983-7 LSB   ISBN 0-671-72984-5   CIP
                                                      AC

Produced by Small Packages, Inc.
Text copyright © 1991 Small Packages, Inc.
and Teddy Slater

Illustrations copyright © 1991 Small Packages, Inc.
and Diane Dawson Hearn.

Published by Silver Press, a division of
Silver Burdett Press, Inc.
Simon & Schuster, Inc.
Prentice Hall Bldg., Englewood Cliffs, NJ 07632.

Printed in the United States of America.

10 9 8 7 6 5 4 3 2 1

Samantha and her mom and dad
went shopping one fine day,
along with brother Beauregard
and great aunt Lula Mae.

Sam ran straight to the candies,
the honey buns, and such.
She reached right out to grab some...

...but her father said,
"Don't touch!"

...and gobbled up
all the jelly beans.

...and tweaked her
brother's cheek.

...and turned out
all the lights.

Which line do you think rhymes with "such"?

. . .but her father said, "Don't touch!"

He pulled her little hand away
and told her to be good.
Sam promised—and she meant it—
that she really, truly would.

Aboard the elevator car,
the doors began to close.
"Hands off!" Sam's brother warned her.
"And watch out for your nose!"

On the second floor, Fine Jewelry,
Sam gazed at the lovely things:
baubles and bangles and necklaces...

. . .and a bright red racing bike.

. . .and a giant purple feather duster.

. . .and gold and silver rings.

. . .and a pair of smelly socks.

Which line rhymes with "things"?

. . .and gold and silver rings!

Sam picked up a glittery pin,
but the clerk said with a frown,
"That pin is quite expensive, dear.
You'd better put it down."

"Come along, Sam," called Lula Mae.
"I need a pretty dress.
Won't you help me pick one out?"
Samantha said, "Oh, yes."

On the third floor, Ladies Wear,
Sam's parents stopped to chat.
While Lula shopped, Samantha browsed. . . .

. . . and tried on two left shoes.

. . . and found this lovely hat.

. . . and bumped into
the Easter Bunny.

. . . and then took
a nap on the floor.

Which line rhymes with "chat"?

. . . and found this lovely hat!

But Lula saw her try it on
and said, "Don't touch that, Sam.
You're getting it all dirty."
Samantha sighed, "Yes, ma'am."

As two big tears rolled down Sam's cheeks,
her mom rushed to her side.
She took one look at Sam's sad face,
and, "Wait right here," she cried.

Then to the fourth floor Sam's mom rode
with a bunch of girls and boys.
The doors opened wide and there they were...

. . .in the Cub Scouts' Clothing Department.

. . .in the middle of a roller rink.

. . .on top of Old Smoky.

. . .in a room full of fabulous toys!

What rhymes with "boys"?

. . . in a room full of fabulous toys!

There were lots of toys to choose from,
and it took Mom quite a while
to make the perfect purchase
guaranteed to make Sam smile.

She took the present back to Sam
and said, "This gift's for you.
After all the *don'ts* you've had today,
it's the least that I can do."

"It isn't big or shiny,
and it didn't cost me much.
But it's awfully soft and cuddly,
and it's made for you to touch!"